WARNING

This book contains sexually explicit scenes and adult language. It may be considered offensive to some readers. This book is for sale to adults ONLY.

* * * * * * * * * * * * * * * * * *

Please store your files wisely where they cannot be accessed by underage readers.

Other Books by Darla Dunbar:

<u>The Romeo Alpha BBW Paranormal Shifter Romance Series</u>

Amanda Walker thinks that she has a normal and boring life. That is until after her 24th birthday. Everything changes when she meets the man who says he was supposed to be her husband. Denying everything the man says, she fights him every step of the way. But after he kidnaps her, Amanda discovers that there are some things about her family that her parents kept a secret all these years. Among the history of the family she learns secrets she thought only happened in story books. Can Amanda tell the difference between truth and lies or is she this mysterious woman that holds the key to a legacy?

<u>Romeo Alpha Blood Lines Romance Series</u>

Twenty-four years have passed in relative peace for Amanda and Romeo. They've raised five children into adulthood and are thoroughly enjoying their lives as the Alpha King and Queen of the werewolves. At twenty-four, Sarina is just stepping into her powers and will be ripe for mating when her birthday comes in two weeks. What no one knows is the danger that lurks just outside their tight knit community. Romeo has made peace with the other clans and has enjoyed that peace, but it will all come crashing down around him when his oldest daughter comes of age to take a mate.

The Alpha Feud BBW Paranormal Shifter Romance Series

Eliza's life consisted of reporting on boring, crowd-pleasing events, like their country livestock fair. With the arrival of two handsome brothers, the lives of Eliza and her best friend, Melissa, are shaken to the core. For Eliza, the arrival of this new man becomes a test of her relationship with her current boyfriend, who she's been happily living with for over six years. Does Hayden, a complete stranger, really wield the power to make Eliza reconsider her relationship with Andrew?

The Alpha Packed BBW Paranormal Shifter Romance Series

Darlene has led a quiet life since suffering through a terrible break-up. She wants nothing more than to spend her time in front of the TV, away from any sort of trouble. But all that goes down the drain when handsome, rugged and rough Idris comes into her life. He is a werewolf on the lookout for his missing pack leader. Darlene quickly finds herself pulled towards this mysterious man and at the same time finds herself falling deeper and deeper into the world of the supernatural.

The Mind Talker Paranormal Romance Series

Ananda finds herself on the run and she's not alone. With help from Jared, a stranger that she just met, the two evade capture by an organization that is intent on hunting her kind. Ananda and Jared are able to read minds. When an unfortunate incident happened involving a disturbed individual that resulted in the death of his schoolmates, the secret organization decided to take action.

<u>The Leather Satchel Paranormal Romance Series</u>

Valtina is stuck in Middle World, unable to pass on to The Afterlife. In order to redeem herself from past deeds done, she must help bring romance back into the world and stop The Dark Side from destroying love in its entirety. Following orders issued by Ladaya and armed with a leather satchel filled with the appropriate tools and weapons, Valtina embraces each mission with enthusiasm.

Get the latest update on new releases from the author at:

https://darladunbar.com/newsletter/

This book is Part Five of "<u>The Daemon Paranormal Romance Chronicles</u>"

Book 1 - The Awakening

Phoebe grew up not knowing her mother. The stranger, Apollo Mikos, claimed to know her mother. After that day, Phoebe's life would change forever.

Book 2 - The Shifter

Phoebe is surprised when her dog, Ace, shows up from nowhere. She is on a mission with Apollo to kill the Qilin. That is the only way that the true leader of daemons will emerge.

Book 3 - Forgotten

Juno has been stirring up trouble that has prolonged the infighting among the daemons. In order to get her to stop, Phoebe agrees to give up a year of her memories. But making deals with a siren is never a good thing. Without her memories, Phoebe's romantic relationship with Supay no longer exists. Instead, she leaves Supay for Apollo.

Book 4 - The Siren's Trap

The unsuspecting couple, Phoebe and Supay, made a deal with Juno to stop the infighting among the daemons. But at what price? An entire year was wiped clean from Phoebe's mind. Now Phoebe was with Apollo. Desperate to get her back, Supay considers Juno's new deal. Is it worth the price to pay for the dubious result? To win back Phoebe's love, Supay will need to be unfaithful to her.

Book 5 - Exposed

Hiding away in Peru, Supay and Phoebe start their own family, away from the chaos and the daemon infighting. Meanwhile, Apollo, heart-broken and lost, is lured into another one of Juno's schemes. Making deals with a siren never turns out right. If Apollo accepts the deal, the love of his life may resent him for the rest of his natural life. If he doesn't take the deal, she is lost to him forever.

Book 6 - The Beginning

As preparations for the war between daemons are underway, everyone must begin to choose. Siding temporarily with Apollo, Juno has a moment to look back on her life and figure out how she arrived at this moment. As she sifts through memories of the past, a specific dark stranger stands out. How far will young Juno go with her new love? More importantly, will her mother, Circe, discover the secret tryst?

Book 7 - The Treachery

Having broken the cardinal rule of the sirens, Juno must take action to save her own life and the life of her unborn child. In order to keep her secret safe from the sisterhood, she must kill her lover and conceal her shame. Will Juno betray the sisterhood and save her lover or will she remain loyal by slaying him instead?

Book 8 - Duplicity

Juno's mother, Circe, discovers her lies and gives her an ultimatum to fix everything. As Juno races against the clock to protect her loved ones from Circe, she makes a final choice that could leave her perpetually unhappy. Left to wander the world alone, Juno realizes that freedom means nothing if there is no one to share it with. The nature of Juno's vendetta—and the means she achieves it with—are finally revealed.

Book 9 - Reconnaissance

As Juno's hunt for the daemon's fortress unfolds, Apollo is left alone wondering if she will truly return to him. Will Juno be able to resist her base instincts? More importantly, will she be able to get to the fortress and return without being spotted? Discover how Juno's stealth mission works out.

Book 10 - The Interrogation

Juno tries to hide her rising fear in the presence of her captors. As her fear mounts, she holds on to the hope that Phoebe or Supay will take pity on her. Before that can happen, she has to come clean to Supay about her past. Could he possibly forgive her for what she has done? Will Juno remain faithful to Apollo or will her siren urges take over? Discover how the confrontation with Supay unfolds.

The Daemon Paranormal Romance Chronicles

Exposed

Book Five

By Darla Dunbar

Copyright Revelry Publishing 2015

Table of Contents

Chapter One

IN PERU, Supay and Phoebe had just welcomed their daughter into the world. The tiny infant was named Irene. To the outside world, the little family seemed like a nexus of harmony. Few outsiders would realize the number of troubles they had gone through in the last few years.

It had all started when Phoebe was approached by Apollo. Raised in foster care, she never knew that she was a daemon. Until that day, Phoebe had made all of her money by telling fortunes. As a daemon, she had a unique talent—her ability was to read people's minds and see what their innermost thoughts were. When Apollo showed up, he needed help finding the Qilin. According to the prophecy, the Qilin would indicate the next great leader or wise man. Apollo had drawn her into the hunt because the Qilin was going under a different name, and he needed someone to read minds in order to find her. Together, they had quickly located the Qilin and started a passionate romance. Before long, it ended. Phoebe discovered at the death of the Qilin that Apollo's talent was to give suggestions or manipulate the minds of other people. Due to this, Phoebe could never truly trust him. She could not be certain that her love for him was not just another manipulation. At the same time, she discovered that her dog was actually a shape shifter known as Supay. Although she had felt betrayed at first, she came to terms with this oddity over time. Supay had become her dog so that he could protect her and hopefully save the Qilin. Although it had not helped the Qilin, his protection had kept her safe.

Phoebe picked up Irene and sat down in the rocking chair. It was so peaceful in the nursery. Before long, Supay would return home. Although the infighting among the daemons had died down, it still caused problems. Supay had been stretched to the maximum of his abilities as he tried to bring peace. Their desire to bring peace had come at a temporary cost; the meddlesome siren, Juno, had agreed to stop causing arguments and fighting among the daemons, provided Phoebe give up her memories. Although Phoebe eventually got those memories back, it had led to a temporary break from Juno.

As Irene fell asleep, Phoebe walked into the living room. She started to sit down when Supay walked in. He immediately came up to her for a kiss.

"How are my lovely ladies today?" he asked. Phoebe held him closer and kissed him back hungrily.

"The little one is fine, but the older one needs some attention," she teased. Supay held her closer. Her scent was enticing. Everywhere he turned in his apartment, he could smell her. Running his fingers through her hair, he pulled her head back for another kiss. The ferocity of her passion surprised him and made him want more. Setting his things down, he looked at her inquisitively.

Slowly, he started to unbutton his jacket and waited for her to respond. When she started to pull off her shirt as well, he was certain. She wanted him.

Quietly, they slipped off their clothes and sank to the floor. Like secret trysts among teenagers, they had to remain quiet and not wake up Irene. Running his finger down her naked body, Supay started to play with her clit. He slipped his fingers inside of her and realized how wet she was.

"Mmm... you know, we could try putting that jade necklace on again," he teased. Reaching onto the table, he wrapped the necklace around her neck. Given to her by the Qilin, it was the only reason she could even have children with him. Without the aid of the fertility talisman, she would never have been able to have children outside of her daemon family.

Phoebe laughed. "Already? We just had a daughter." She rocked her hips against his in an effort to bring him into her.

Supay smiled and pulled his hips away. He could just as easily keep her waiting for more. While he spent the day tirelessly working, she had spent it thinking about him. He knew that this would make it easy for him to torture her with a brief wait. When she insisted on sex, it turned him on. He loved making her demand it.

"Yes, we have a daughter. Still, it is not like it was that easy to have children. We have to start trying again if we plan on having all ten." He smiled.

"Ten!" Phoebe laughed. "Now I know you're joking. This isn't ancient Peru or Greece. What would we do with ten?"

He shrugged. "Build our own daemon peacekeeping force. Think about it. With your genetics and mine, they're bound to be extra powerful. At the very least, they will probably end up with multiple abilities."

Phoebe tried to change the subject. She just wanted him inside of her. All day, she had waited for this exact moment. Pulling the necklace on, she showed it to him. "See? Now will you have sex with me?"

Supay pretended to think about it. Beneath him, Phoebe squirmed and tried to get him inside of her. Laughing, he entered her without warning. The sudden pleasure made him gasp. Her soft hips were receptive to him and opened to take him in further. He could almost feel the sexual desire oozing out of her body.

Phoebe pushed Supay onto the ground and got on top of him. Grabbing her shirt from the floor, she used it to tie his hands. "There, now you cannot stop me." Triumphant, she pushed her body down onto his. The angle of her position caused his body to press against her clit. Moaning, she started to move in time with him. As her moans started to increase, Supay sat up and tried to cover her mouth. Instead she placed her mouth on his shoulder. Every time she wanted to moan, she bit into him. He slid effortlessly into her because of her wetness. Seeing that he was past the point of no return, she undid his restraints. As she did so, he grabbed her hips and pulled her onto him. Standing up, he pressed her against the wall hard. Entering her completely, Supay gasped as he realized he was starting to orgasm. It was impossible that he was already, but she felt so good around him that he could not stop. After orgasm, he kept going. Unless she came as well, he was not going to stop.

His cock was sensitive as he continued. The amount of pleasure that was moving through his body was almost painful. Around him, Phoebe started to shake. She bit her lip as she tried to hold back a moan, but it was impossible. Her orgasm was felt audibly and physically by Supay. As she finished, the baby started crying in the other room. Laughing again, Supay put on his pants.

"Well, we tried not to wake her. I'll go put her back to sleep." Pushing his fingers between her legs, he felt how wet she was. For a moment, he wanted to ignore the baby and go at it again. Struggling to focus, his cock jerked. He pushed her legs open and entered her quickly. Knowing that there was little time and unable to control his desire, he pushed violently into her. Her back started to bruise as he thrust harder and harder against her. Pain and pleasure intermingled as he was pushed to the brink. Before his eyes, there was nothing. Passion had blinded him and deafened him. He could not see or do anything other than feel his hardness surrounded by her wet softness. He came again inside her with a groan that would certainly have woken any neighbors. Reluctantly, he pulled himself out of her.

Leaving the room, he went to take care of Irene. Phoebe shook slightly from the violence and passion of their lovemaking. She still wanted more. After Irene was asleep, she would bring him to her again.

Chapter Two

While Phoebe and Supay were enjoying family life, Apollo was not quite so lucky. Depressed about losing Phoebe, he had taken to spending his afternoons and evenings in a bar. It was not an exciting life, but it was all he had the willpower to do. Once, he had almost killed himself. Alone at home, he had taken out a gun and considered firing it into his skull. As soon as that thought crossed his mind, he remembered stories of people who did not die from head wounds. He shuddered to think about what life would be like if he was mentally incapacitated or a vegetable. Not only that, but shooting himself was the coward's way out. He could do better than that.

Despite his depression, he knew that things were going well for Supay and Phoebe. It only made his pain worse. He had heard through the grapevine about Supay's efforts to end the daemon fighting. As soon as he heard about it, he realized that the prophecy had been correct. The death of the Qilin had shown a great leader. Apollo may have killed the Qilin, but the great leader was Supay. By saving Phoebe and trying to avoid the crush of fate, he had proven himself to be worthy of a leadership role. He had his problems like everyone, but these issues had only made him a better leader. Even now, the disputes and troubles in the daemon world were coming to a close. Everyone except Apollo seemed to be getting a happily-ever-after story.

Sipping some whiskey, he watched as the Peruvian news station appeared. It was pathetic, but he had moved to Peru to be closer to Phoebe. To prevent it from being pathetically noticeable, he chose to live in Lima instead of Cuzco. It was still pathetic, but at least it made his situation seem like he could have just been there by chance. He had tried hiking to Macchu Picchu and even spent a few weeks with a shaman, but nothing seemed to take his mind off of his current situation.

Turning around, he watched as a raven black haired woman entered the bar. From the movement of her hips to the pout of her lips, every movement exuded sexual desire. Within seconds, Apollo groaned. It was Juno.

He pulled out a seat for her and ordered a drink for each of them as she came up. Juno reacted with mock surprise. "Why, what a welcome. Normally people run when I approach, but you invite me closer." She bounced onto the bar stool effortlessly.

"There isn't any point to ignoring you; it just makes you happier." Apollo grimaced and took a sip of his whiskey.

"Ah, there's the man I love. You know me so well, Apollo. It's a shame we haven't worked together before this." She dimpled innocently for him.

Apollo shook his head. "I know better than to deal with a siren. It doesn't matter how good the deal seems, you always have the upper hand. As a siren, all you care about is causing havoc and broken hearts anywhere you go."

"True, so maybe I should just leave without making you my offer?" Smiling seductively, she played with her necklace. The movement around her necklace drew his eyes down to her breasts.

"Nice try. I don't care for your games. I'm also not stupid enough to send you away. The only thing worse than dealing with a siren is hurting one."

Juno leaned forward until her lips were just grazing the edge of his ear. "There's a smart boy." She pulled back and glanced at him. "Well, if you don't want to deal, we can always just catch up on our lives."

Apollo snorted. "Do you have a life outside of ruining the lives of other people?"

Juno spun around on her bar stool. Stopping the spinning with her foot, she giggled. "I wouldn't say that I ruin them. Besides, there is nothing that I could do to make your life worse."

"Thanks for reminding me," Apollo responded dryly. He ran his fingers through his messed-up blonde hair. "So I guess we're already caught up then. You know everything that is happening in my life."

Juno spun the stool around again. "Not quite," she said in a singsong voice. "I know who ruined it, but I am bound not to tell." Her musical voice drifted into the noisy bar.

Apollo glanced at her. "What do you mean 'who ruined it'? Obviously, Supay ruined it." There was a pause and Juno did not respond. Apollo's eyes widened and he grabbed her by her throat. Choking her neck, he managed to squeeze out a sentence with effort. "What... do... you... know?"

Pushing him off of her, Juno gasped for breath. Her face transformed for a moment from a sultry goddess into a mask of pure anger and fury. Calming herself, she slipped back into her normal role. "That wasn't very nice. Now I may not tell you. I can't really tell you anyhow." She brushed herself off.

Apollo was starting to see red. His entire field of vision was swimming due to anger. "What do you know?"

Juno shrugged and reached for her bag. Apollo shoved her hand away and grabbed her wrist to stop her from leaving. No longer angry, Juno started to feel pleased with herself again. She may finally be able to get what she wanted. It looked like he was ready to deal. She sat back on the bar stool and took a sip of her drink.

"Well, I have something that would interest you and change your fortunes around. The only problem is that I cannot tell anyone. You could, however, do your mind manipulation and make me tell you the information."

"What would stop me from doing that anyhow?"

Juno laughed. "Honey, we already covered this. You don't mess with a siren. I'll ruin your life even more just for the hell of it."

Sighing, Apollo thought about it. "What do you want from me? You always seem to leave more ruin behind in these deals than benefits."

Winking, Juno patted his hand. "Cross my heart, this deal is only going to help you or leave you the same. Others may have their lives harmed, so that will be the only pleasure I can take out of this. There is one thing you can do."

Apollo waited. Juno did not say anything. Instead she lowered her gaze and batted her eyes. Groaning, Apollo shook his head.

Juno frowned. "It isn't like it is a serious issue for you. Now and again, I like to have sex."

"But why me? Walk up to any guy here and have sex with him."

Shrugging, Juno smiled. "Two reasons. The first issue is that they are too easy. My personality may turn them off, but they just don't have the willpower to fight my machinations. The second reason? It pleases me to make you do something that reviles you so much, yet still turns you on. My needs are quite basic."

Motioning to the bartender, Apollo ordered another drink. He took a deep breath. "So how will this work? You got a hotel room or something?"

Picking up his hand, Juno placed her mouth around his finger. Watching her lips around him turned him on, despite his desire to ignore her. Letting his hand go, Juno shrugged. "We can carry out this arrangement here, in a hotel, in your apartment, or in the parking lot. I really don't care too much." She paused. "Actually, do you have a car?"

Apollo groaned. "I shouldn't have even asked you that question. Yes, I have a car. Let's go outside."

Walking outside together, he opened the door for her. Juno shook her head and pointed to the backseat. Simultaneously hating himself and wanting this to be over, he opened the back door and crawled in with her. Without a word, she started to take his shirt off and kissed along his clavicle. Her hands moved down his body and she felt how hard he was.

"You can't help genetics, can you? You may hate me, but it doesn't stop you from wanting me," she grinned.

Wanting her to shut up, he put one hand around her throat. With his other hand, he covered her mouth. "No talking," he whispered.

Letting go of her neck, he unzipped his pants. His manhood immediately stood up to attention. Smiling, Juno slipped out of her jeans and spread her legs. The front seat stopped her from opening her legs all the way. Outside, the light was starting to dim as sunset approached. Passerby would still be able to see a car rocking, but were less likely to see exactly what was going on inside. Reaching her hand toward him, she stroked him. He tried to enter her and end this charade, but she would not let him. Stroking his flesh, she made him harder than before. He quivered with desire and hated that his body had betrayed him in this way. Before him, her body stretched supply. Her shirt strained just enough around her breasts to hint at what lay beneath. He guessed that she was not wearing a bra because even now, her nipples stood visibly up through the shirt. Suddenly, Apollo was overcome with desire. He wanted to see her breasts and naked body in its entirety. Reaching for her shirt, he tried to pull it off, but she stopped him. A denial was not going to work for him. Using both hands, he ripped her shirt apart. Both breasts popped out invitingly. Holding her down, Apollo massaged each breast before taking her nipple into his mouth. After fighting him to slow down, Juno lay back and let him lick hungrily at her body.

His hatred of her was not enough to stop him from wanting to take her body and own it. Apollo's body quivered with anticipation, but she forced him away. Later, she wanted him to think back and remember that he forced her. She wanted him to know that he had sex with someone that he despised and that it was ultimately his choice. This power over him aroused her. Without thinking about it, she gave in and let him run his fingers along her wetness. As her desire increased, she opened her legs again for him to enter. He did not have to think twice. Within seconds, he was in her and pumping against her svelte figure. His knee hit awkwardly against the front seat, but he did not care anymore. Nothing mattered except being inside her and feeling her around him. Thrusting harder, he could feel her coming close to orgasm. Uninhibited, she started to cry out and moan in pleasure. The sound of her moaning brought him to orgasm. Drawing her nails along his back, she scratched him as she came.

Falling backward, she held his head to her body. Apollo let her run her fingers through his hair for a moment before he started crying quietly. A mixture of longing, disgust, and self-pity had finally overwhelmed him. He did not care who it was, he just needed human contact. Without Phoebe, he had no one in his life. Lifting his head, he dragged his teeth along her body. He wanted inside of her again. The momentary reprieve from his life was not enough. He needed to be inside her. Smiling, Juno allowed him to enter her again. This second time was less violent and more loving. For some reason, it felt right. Pulling out after orgasm, he struggled to get his jeans back on. Juno threw her motorcycle jacket over her bare breasts.

"Keep the shirt," she said, motioning to the ripped up shreds. "You ruined it anyhow."

Apollo looked at her. "Is this really who you are? Just because you are a siren does not mean you have to act like one. You could be your own person."

Juno laughed and kissed his lips. Biting on his lip, she pulled away. "I'm not pretending to be anything. This is who I am. Besides, you are the one who believes so much in fate. This is my role to play and I enjoy it."

Sighing, Apollo pulled his shirt on. For a moment, he had felt like she was a different person, like something was opening up within her. The moment had passed, and now he was just disgusted again. "So now I get to see the big secret that you have hyped up, correct?" She nodded.

Reaching for her arm, Apollo planted the suggestion that she should tell him in her brain. At first, her mind would not allow it. Trying again, he managed to break through the barriers and get her to open up. Robotically, she started to speak. "Supay wanted Phoebe back. In trade for sex, I gave him a spell that would make her love him. If she discovers the spell has been placed, it will break. She can love him, but never the same."

Apollo paused. "Wait, how did he know that you wouldn't just turn around and tell me?"

As if under hypnosis, Juno answered. "It was part of the deal. I could never tell anyone." Her body was completely frozen as her mind processed his requests.

"But you told me..." His eyes widened. "You knew I could make your mind tell me. You never really made the deal with him because you knew you could get around it."

Juno nodded. "I'm a siren." The way she said it indicated that she considered the matter closed.

Since she had already submitted to his mind control, Apollo decided to continue questioning her. "So what is it you want out of me? If I tell them, I don't lose in any way."

Nodding again, Juno started to speak. "You're right, but they will lose if you tell them and they stay together or if they separate. If this does not work for you, you have to be with someone."

Apollo looked at her inquisitively. "Someone?"

"Yes, someone. A long time ago, I made a deal with an Indian prophet. He told me that without Phoebe's sister being born, you or Supay would end up being with me. It wasn't what was fated, but it was the only possible result now."

Pulling away from her, Apollo reacted with shock. "You? And me? That's impossible." As he pulled away, he lost the connection with her and she reverted to her normal self.

Smiling, Juno leaned over to kiss him on the cheek. "It may be impossible, but one of you will be with me. Think of it. If you don't get Phoebe, you'll want to be with someone. Since she was your soul mate, you don't really care about who. And as a siren, I will stay young and beautiful all my life. You might hate me, but you could do worse."

Stumbling backward, Apollo reached for the door of the car. "Leave. Just leave."

Smiling, she zipped up her jacket. "When you change your mind, call me." She dropped her number on the hood of the car. Apollo tossed it into the passenger seat.

Juno sauntered off and got on her motorcycle. Getting in the driver's seat, Apollo tried to control his shaking hands. He did not want Juno to be his future. It was impossible. He had to see Phoebe as soon as possible to see if he could change it. If he was lucky, Supay would be gone and he would be able to see her alone. Apollo started the car to go see Phoebe. Driving along the open highway, he only stopped to buy coffee. Before seeing Juno, he had spent several weeks on an alcohol bender and missed out on a lot of sleep. He would not be looking his best for Phoebe, but he hoped it would work out. Nothing seemed to go according to plan, but he still could wish for things to turn out right.

Chapter Three

From outside the apartment, Apollo tried his hand on the handle. He did not want to knock and have Supay answer. Everything would go better if he could just slip inside and see if Supay was there with her. Quietly, he turned the handle and opened the door inch by inch. Creeping into the apartment, he caught sight of Phoebe in the kitchen and stepped back. She was humming a song from the radio as she made dinner. When her back was turned, he admired her in secret. Here was the love of his life. This had to go better than he had hoped.

In the kitchen, Phoebe was almost done making dinner when she heard something in the living room. Turning around, she saw Apollo standing there. His eyes were haggard and he held up his hands defensively. For a moment, she almost pitied him. This temporary sensation of pity was quickly driven away by her anger at him suddenly appearing in her apartment.

"Look, I know you don't want to see me. If you ask me to, this will be the last time." He waited for her response. For a brief period of time, it looked like she would throw him out without saying anything. When she did not automatically kick him out, he let out his breath; without realizing it, he had been holding his breath as he waited for her response.

Sitting down at the table, Phoebe took a deep breath. "Okay, that's fine. Considering we both just left in Spain, that seems like a reasonable request. What did you want?"

Pulling out the chair across from her, Apollo sat down and relayed everything that Juno told him. Except for having sex with her, he recounted every piece of the tale. He tried not to sound spiteful or vindictive, but the topic of Supay did not sit well with him. Even before Phoebe, he had not liked Supay because Supay was trying to stop him from killing the Qilin. Unfortunately Supay had been right, which only made his hatred worse.

As he finished, something broke within Phoebe. She had spent too long trying to figure out her life. At this point, she was just tired of having to change or learning about new betrayals. She could not take this style of living any longer. It had to end. She had to figure out some way to make her life work and stop changing everything. This had to happen for Phoebe, but also for Irene. Irene deserved to have a stable childhood and a loving family.

Trying to figure out the entire story, she started to review everything in her mind. Confused, she looked up at Apollo. "So you told me, which means the love spell is broken, right?"

Apollo nodded and waited with bated breath.

"You ruined my happiness in the hopes that it would make me return to you?" Her anger was starting to become apparent. Too late, Apollo realized that he had made a mistake.

"I thought you deserved to know. And..." he stuttered, "... and I love you. I just did it because I wanted to be with you." He paused again. "I guess I wasn't thinking." Apollo hung his head in dismay. His plan had completely backfired. Not only did he not get Phoebe, but he had just ruined a part of her life. He cursed himself silently. Dealing with sirens never turned out well. If he had not wanted Phoebe so much, he would not have let a siren convince him to do this. To make the situation worse, he realized too late that Juno had lied. His life could become more miserable. He could end up without Phoebe and with the knowledge that he had hurt the one woman that he had ever loved.

Standing up, Phoebe started to pace the room. Rubbing her temples, she tried to think. If she stayed with Supay, she would never be able to love him completely in the way she was supposed to. Being with Apollo disgusted her now. She could leave Supay and hope to find someone else, but that seemed impossible. Phoebe still loved him and wanted to help him lead the daemon world towards peace. Even more so, she had started to believe that there was some type of fate guiding her actions. The Qilin had marked the way of a great leader. Pausing, she looked back at Apollo. Anger flashed in her eyes, but she kept her attitude calm in order to get more information from him.

"Wait, she didn't say that I couldn't love him or be in love with him, right?" She waited patiently for him to answer.

Apollo shrugged awkwardly. He wished he could just leave now. "No, she just said it would stop you from having true love."

"And it wouldn't change how Supay feels?" she asked.

Apollo shook his head. He already saw where this was going. If it would not hurt Phoebe, he would kill Supay. Effortlessly, Supay had managed to take his goal of being a leader and the potential love of his life away. Under the table, his fists clenched with pent-up rage.

"Then I want you to leave before Supay comes home. And I never want to see you again." Turning her back, she waited for him to leave.

After Apollo left, she went into the nursery to look at her sleeping child. She would never be able to love Supay as fully as before, but he would never know that. There may be days where he felt something was off, but he would still love her all the same. In her sleep, Irene let out a little cry. Singing a nursery song, Phoebe sat by her as Irene fell back into a deep sleep. Nothing would change. Nothing.

-To be continued in Book 6-

If you enjoyed this title, I would appreciate your leaving a review of the book. Good reviews encourage an author to write as well as help books to sell. Good reviews can be just a few short sentences describing what you liked about the book without having a spoiler. If you could spend 30 seconds writing a review, I would appreciate it: you can review this title right now at your favorite retailer.

Here is a preview of the **next story** you may enjoy:

The Beginning - The Daemon Paranormal Romance Chronicles, Book 6

THE CALL of an archer could be heard on the battlement. Juno snorted. It wasn't really by choice that she was here with the Romans. Unlike other daemons, she had no allegiance. Although the majority of sirens were part of the Greek tribe of daemons, sirens were not creatures that claimed allegiance to everything. She had, unfortunately, ended up here because of outside circumstances.

Not long ago, she had created a careful plan to wreck the life of Phoebe Williams. At the time, she had hoped that it would bring Supay back to her. That had never materialized and she had instead been left with Apollo. Like her, he had been left without a daemon tribe. After her last attempt at breaking Supay and Phoebe apart, Apollo had been left to suffer from the fall out. He had hoped that Phoebe would choose him in the end. When she had not, he had thrown all of his efforts behind the Roman tribe. They were a rough and tumble bunch, but he no longer seemed to care. Instead, Apollo had quickly developed a singular focus on revenge. Juno had thrown her lot in with Apollo out of the hope that something would jar Supay out of his sickeningly complacent relationship with Phoebe.

Gazing back at the archers, Juno just shook her head. The slight tilt of her chin caused her straight black hair to sway back and forth. Her overly large eyes narrowed uncharacteristically as she tried to hide her annoyance at the Romans. For some reason, they seemed to think that this daemon war was a medieval battlefield. Over the last few months, they had started building supplies and weapons at this lonely base in Sicily. Since she had sworn to stay out of the fight due to her agreement with Phoebe, Juno could not step in and show them how they were doing it wrong. For starters, they had placed the archers on the lowest wall. As the easiest location to climb, the lowest wall would be better suited to giant vats of tar and boulders. Other than a complete lack of knowledge in this field, the Romans also lacked the ability to see that they would be easily routed. Although modern weapons and techniques drew more public attention to the daemon wars, they were also more effective.

Sniffing disdainfully, Juno went back into the castle. She may have promised not to actively fight, but that didn't mean that she could not remain up-to-date on the latest happenings in the daemon world. Purposefully navigating the corridors of the castle, she began to climb the narrow stairs that led to the north tower. With its poorly made steps and drafty interior, few people bothered to enter this part of the castle. This one fact made it perfect for her use.

Entering the tower, Juno set about closing the curtains. At the last curtain, she stopped and peered out at the ground. Below her, Apollo was shouting orders as he tried to get the troops in line. As she watched him, Juno felt a stirring of something within her heart. Not long ago, she had convinced Apollo to sleep with her. Although he had been appalled at the idea when she asked, he had readily returned to her bed since that time. Juno sighed. The life of a siren was never easy. Long ago, she had planned out a different, beautiful life for herself. Since that time, everything had gone wrong and now she was just another siren operating in a chaotic world.

Approaching the sink, she filled several pitchers with water. Each time one pitcher filled, she brought it to the table and used it to fill up a scrying basin. Circular and sleek, the ebony marble gleamed in the evening light. In just a few moments, she would use it to gaze across the world to watch the enemy at work.

Sitting at the table, Juno began to focus her mind. The clutter of her thoughts would not quiet readily, so she leaned back with a sigh. If she could not watch the Greeks mount an attack or Supay attempt to stop the battle, she should do something else. Her mind wandered as she thought about what she needed. After all this time, she had allotted very few moments to herself. Her rosebud lips pursed slightly before relaxing into a grin. Yes, this was just the time for her to revisit her past. A reminder of how she arrived at this place in life would be just the thing that she needed to renew her focus. Settling into the chair further, she waved her hand confidently across the water of the scrying tub. As the ripples expanded outward, pictures began to reveal themselves.

Across the field, a young, beautiful girl darted among the sheep. The dappled sunlight on the ground jostled merrily as the leaves moved in time with each gust of the breeze. Gorgeous and strangely innocent, the young girl fell next to the herd of sheep after a stray rock tripped her up. Laughing prettily, she shook out her straight black hair from a messy bun. The raven black hair fell neatly on her back as she gently combed her fingers through it. Gazing out at the sheep, young Juno knew that there were few better places to be in the world.

Each morning, she picked up her crook and a loaf of bread before heading out toward the Andes. Over recent years, her tribe of sirens had settled down in the area. Known for causing trouble, they never stayed anywhere for more than five or ten years. This time, Juno wanted them to stay. She loved waking up to the smell of coffee brewing and wandering the fields with her sheep. Her mother, Circe, had given her this task to keep her out of trouble. Until her nineteenth birthday, Juno was an untrained siren. Unfamiliar with the ways of the world or sirens, she was told to keep herself out of mischief. As a shepherdess, it would be next to impossible to get into trouble. Honestly, Juno preferred her life this way. None of the sirens like her Aunt Pasiphae or her mother were ever happy. They pretended to be happy and were certainly charming, but the siren way of life tended to be a lonely one. Men were taken and used, but never kept, and love was forbidden. According to her mother, it was impossible for a siren to ever become anything else.

Leaning back into the sweet meadow grass, Juno relaxed luxuriously on her arms. The noonday sun beat above her head and reminded her that it was time for lunch. Rolling over, she reached for her pack and pulled out the loaf of bread. It would be eaten with a small jug of milk. She sighed and her dainty eyelashes drooped slightly. The jug of milk was leaking again. Today would be another day that she would go home starving.

Just as Juno was about to begin her lunch, she heard a noise at the far end of the meadow. Some of her sheep were darting out of the way, as strange sheep approached. Standing up quickly, Juno dropped the loaf of bread on the ground. Cursing at her stupidity, she leaned down to pick it up. With her intent focus on cleaning the bread, she almost forgot about the strange sheep. She glanced up just in time to see a large, black dog dart into view. It seemed intent on herding the sheep into the meadow until it caught sight of her. The sudden shock of seeing someone else caused the dog to lose focus. Before Juno's eyes, the black canine transformed into the naked form of a young man.

Her almond eyes opened widely. "Sir...?" she asked curiously.

Groaning in embarrassment, the young man reached around for something to cover himself with. Juno realized his shame and smiled. Unwrapping the shawl around her waist, she tossed it over to him. Grinning bashfully, the young man tied it around his waist and walked over.

He reached out his hand. "Hi, I'm Supay. I... well. I apologize. This doesn't normally happen. Surprises still jolt me out of shape shifting. I'm still learning. What's your name?"

Juno smiled prettily and stretched out her thin, delicate hand. "I'm Juno. Don't worry about your mistake. I think you're the first person I've seen up here in months and the first man I've seen at all in years."

Supay tilted his head. "What do you mean? How could you not see a man for years?"

If you enjoyed this sample then look for **The Beginning - The Daemon Paranormal Romance Chronicles, Book 6**.

Here is a preview of the **next story** you may enjoy:

Evasion - The Mind Talker Paranormal Romance Series, Book 5

JARED FELT anything but relaxed as he sat across from the man who just introduced himself as Ananda's older brother. Typically, he would assume a first meeting with the family of a significant other would include a semi-awkward dinner with the father asking all sorts of probing questions followed by pseudo threats of death by shotgun if a hair on his darling daughter's head was out of place. Instead Jared sat gingerly on the edge of a raggedy bed, clothes having been hastily pulled on in the wake of their new company, with Ananda sobbing in her big brother's arms. A big brother who somehow managed to be comforting to his sister while his eyes promised swift and sudden death to Jared if he found she had come to any harm.

Ananda missed the exchange between her brother and Jared as she pulled back, tears in her eyes and a sob stuck in her throat. Truthfully she had thought she would never see Ryan again and was a bit perplexed by his abrupt re-entry into her life. Her gaze was drawn to how close Ryan and Kerrie were as well as the feeling of raw magnetism that almost radiated between them. Slowly, she backed away until Jared guided her down until she was almost perched across his lap, his arm never leaving the place where it was draped across her waist in a possessive and comforting hold.

"I'm…" Ananda, swallowed hard pushing down the lump in her throat. "It's been months, Ryan. Months! One minute you're telling me about your exploits in the real world; job, house, car, everything. The next you just up and disappear with no phone calls, no emails, nothing!"

"I know Ana and I'm sorry, I really am but," Ryan paused, his gaze sliding over to Kerri as if needing her permission to speak the truth. Ananda could feel her fury rising over her brother and best friend's seemingly unspoken exchange. "We wanted to keep you safe –"

"Keep me safe?!" Ananda exclaimed incredulously. "Were you keeping me safe when you let mom and dad send me to all those shrinks and specialists who made me feel as if I were crazy for hearing voices? Were you keeping me safe when you abandoned me and moved halfway across the country the first chance you got?!" Ananda's voice rang out shrilly as she stood abruptly, fists balled and barely hanging onto what little sanity she had left after the past few days.

"Ananda I know," Ryan started only to be cut off again by his sister's angry voice.

Fighting against Jared's tightening hold around her waist, Ananda could feel fresh hot tears spilling from her eyes and racing down her flushed cheeks. "No you don't Ryan. You don't know shit about anything, especially not how I feel. And you," Ananda turned to the woman she had loved as a sister sitting stock still and unsurprised by Ananda's ire. Her unusual calm almost made Ananda want to rage even harder. "I thought you were my friend and now it seems you'd been lying to me too. How long have you two been plotting and spying on me, huh? Did you have a good laugh at my bumbling efforts to figure out who I was? I should have known something wasn't right when you never invited me to meet your family!"

At the mention of her family, Kerri's countenance changed and her words rang out with a fury greater than Ananda had ever witnessed from the redhead.

"My family is the reason why our lives are so fucked right now!" Kerri used her hands to say the word family in quotations as if the very idea of family was somehow ridiculous. "The reason I've never invited you to meet them is because I washed my hands of them years ago." The slight woman stood abruptly and began pacing as if unable to speak the words while staying still.

"When I was fifteen, my mother, younger sister and I moved to New York. I thought it was strange that my father and brothers didn't come with us, but I figured he had a good reason and didn't dwell on it, instead focusing on school and making friends and trying to be popular." Kerri stopped, turning slowly to look at Ryan, emotion clear in her eyes. "And then I fell in love."

Blinking, Jared looked between the two guests. Without even trying, he could feel the love and affection that practically pulsed off of the two in waves and wondered if he and Ananda were exuding similar feelings.

"I'm so confused right now," Ananda whispered plopping down beside Jared once again. She leaned against him heavily and gladly soaked up the feelings of calm the man was radiating out. She would have had to be a fool to not see the depth of feeling between her brother and Kerri, but it still didn't explain how they knew each other or why they were here now. And how did they even find them?

"I called Bill, whose real name is apparently Ryan and he is also, apparently, your brother," Jared answered.

"Wait," Ananda spoke up. "Didn't you say your friend Bill was in Canada? Wasn't he the guy with safe houses?"

If you enjoyed this sample then look for **Evasion - The Mind Talker Paranormal Romance Series, Book 5**.

Here is a preview of **another story** you may enjoy:

Valtina's Redemption - The Leather Satchel Paranormal Romance Series, Book 1

NOT EVERYONE was given a second chance, especially after failing so many times before. Valtina was among the lucky few who got a real opportunity to redeem themselves. She was a spirit trapped in The Middle World: a place filled with souls who have gone astray and were not granted entrance into The Afterlife until they have learned a few lessons and found their place. These were lost souls in a way, and Valtina was most likely just a lifetime away from discovering her true identity. Right now, however, she was summoned by Ladaya to discuss a task that may grant her access to The Afterlife if she can complete it successfully. Valtina waited hopefully for her to arrive.

Ladaya has already perfected her soul. She has earned her place in The Afterlife, but she has also learned what it means to help others, and so she returned regularly to guide souls through their journey and to help them succeed on their own paths. Now, she coalesced out of the gray fog surrounding them. Valtina's face lit up with excitement and a hint of nervousness. Thoughts flooded her mind of the different jobs she may be asked to complete, and she was worried that they may not be things she herself can do. Nevertheless, she held her composure, hopeful that she might be reunited with her family and lovers in The Afterlife.

"Hello, Valtina," Ladaya smiled warmly at her.

"Hello."

"Thank you for agreeing to meet me today… I really need your help. If you can do this successfully, I'll reward you in the fullest. It will be worth it in more ways than one, trust me."

"I'm happy to help, but what exactly do you want me to do?"

"Given the grave matter we are dealing with, I am going to need to leave a lot of the decision making to you. But I'll give you a bit of background information to get you started. As you may have noticed in your last life, the world is on a decline, especially in the area of love. Couples are no longer able to love each other the way that they should. Cheating is becoming a normal thing—many partners are having extramarital affairs and sleeping with multiple women while trying to keep up the appearance that they are 'dedicated' to their wives or girlfriend. Even more couples are only staying together because of lust, and no other attraction towards the other person. They don't love each other and their relationships are meaningless.

"This might not seem like a huge problem at first, but the entire universe is based on love and human compassion. That's something that we can't survive without, and evil is tempting people away from their core values. It won't take long before the world is in tatters and everything will fall apart. Now, this is where you come in."

"I'm going to need you to help breathe life and passion back into relationships that have gone stale and started to fall apart. Over the centuries, I've seen how you are in each life that you have lived. You are dripping with sexual energy and you have had some of the most successful relationships that I've ever seen. I know that you can do this job. I need you to do this for me."

Valtina pondered this for a few moments, doubting whether or not she would be able to successfully do the task expected of her. Even though she may have been able to understand everything in the world, she had always been successful in her love life, in every life. She felt confident with the idea that she won't have to save any lives or stop a bombing or anything complicated like that. She smiled as she realized that this could actually be a fun thing for her and she was practically beaming as she started to speak, "Alright, I'll do it. Where should I start?"

"Well, to begin with, there's a couple that we know who are truly meant to be together. Their names are Samantha and Joshua. They recently got married—only 4 years ago. Already, their sex lives are deteriorating. I want you to fix this. They haven't been intimate in months. Although I'm not entirely sure why this is, I know that they both would be interested in trying some light bondage and they'll be much better off with a change of pace."

She smiled more, realizing that she would be in her element throughout this job. "Sounds good… I can do that, no problem."

"For you to use, I want you to take this leather satchel. It contains some of the most important things that will help you work with these couples. I'm also going to give you some basic abilities that will help you read their minds or redirect their thoughts; inspire them though, don't take control."

"Sure thing."

"I believe in you, Valtina. I know that you will save us."

<<◇>>

Valtina dissolved into the fog and reappeared in a modest apartment. The room was filled with photographs and cozy-looking furniture. In an armchair, Joshua was sitting on his own while his wife was curled up on the couch at the other side of the living room. Valtina stood there taking in the scene, saddened to see a married couple sitting apart when they would obviously be more comfortable sitting together.

A few moments after Valtina got there, as she continued taking in her surroundings, the man stood up and stretched. He yawned, "Honey, I'm going to bed. Are you coming with me?"

It took a moment for Samantha to answer. She was zoned out, staring blankly at the television. "Oh, no, not right now. I think I'm going to read for a while and take a shower first. Have a good night." As she talked, she leaned forward and opened up a book from the coffee table.

"Alright, have a good night. I love you."

She didn't answer; she was already pretending to be absorbed in the words on the page in front of her. Even Joshua knew that she heard but chose to ignore him. Valtina was already starting to worry that this job might be harder than she expected as she watched Joshua walk slowly to the bedroom and Samantha sit on the couch, resolved to making him miserable and prolonging her misery. This brief scene was an obvious representation of the heartache that was here.

It was clear that all Joshua wanted was to be closer to this wife, and that was understandable. After all, who wouldn't? With the abilities that Valtina had, she knew that he had been trying for months to improve things with her, but Samantha wasn't willing to do anything else. She was bored and it was clear that things needed to change.

Valtina understood both sides of the situation. Joshua loved his wife and he wanted to make her happy, but he clearly didn't know how. Samantha still loved her husband, but after doing the exact same thing for so long, it was hard to be passionate about vanilla sex. As she considered this, Valtina decided that she will have to start work first thing in the morning.

If you enjoyed this sample then look for **Valtina's Redemption - The Leather Satchel Paranormal Romance Series, Book 1**.

Other Books by Darla Dunbar

- The Romeo Alpha BBW Paranormal Shifter Romance Series

- Romeo Alpha Blood Lines Romance

- The Alpha Feud BBW Paranormal Shifter Romance Series

- The Alpha Packed BBW Paranormal Shifter Romance Series

- The Mind Talker Paranormal Romance Series

- The Leather Satchel Paranormal Romance Series

Get the latest update on new releases from the author at:

https://darladunbar.com/newsletter/

About the Author - Darla Dunbar

Darla has been interested in paranormal romance since she was a teenager in high school. It was then that she discovered she could fulfill her fantasies through her writing.

Observing people and human behavior in the area of romance has always been one of her favorite pastimes. Combining that with an overactive imagination is a sure fire way of coming up with interesting themes.

Connect with Darla Dunbar

I really appreciate you reading my book! Here are my social media coordinates:

Friend me on Facebook: https://www.facebook.com/darladunbar/

Follow me on Twitter: https://twitter.com/DarlDunbar

Check me out on Goodreads: https://www.goodreads.com/author/show/8425857.Darla_Dunbar

Subscribe to my newsletter: https://darladunbar.com/newsletter/

Visit my website: https://darladunbar.com/